No Pig's Brain Soup, Please!

written by
Gail Greenberg

Illustrated by
Lauren Forgie

Published by
Kam Publishing, LP
959 Knight Drive
Durant, OK 74701
www.llibs.com

Cover Designed by Ira S. Van Scoyoc
Book designed by Ira S.Van Scoyoc and Pam Van Scoyoc
Edited by Pam Van Scoyoc
Printed in the United States of America

Cataloging in Publication Data
Greenberg, Gail, 1955-
No pig's brain soup, please! / written by Gail Greenberg ; illustrated by Lauren Forgie.
    p. cm.
Summary: Tali, a young Chinese girl who was adopted as an infant by Jewish American parents,
struggles with conflicts of culture, customs, and identity on her school's International Night.
An authentic recipe is included.
ISBN 978-0-9795474-3-0 (hardback)
1. Chinese American children – Juvenile literature. 2. Jewish Children – United States – Juvenile
literature. 3. Food in popular culture. [1. Adoption – Fiction.] I. Forgie, Lauren, ill. II. Title.

PZ7.G8274
813 [Fic]
Library of Congress Control Number: 2008936516

To my daughter, Hayley, who is my greatest treasure.

To Pam for her countless time, knowledge, and help in getting this book published.

To my critique groups for their encouragement, and feedback.

To my family and friends for their support. I love you all.

Gail

To my mother Patricia Both.

Lauren

Many Jewish people only eat meat from certain animals. This is called Kosher and is according to Jewish law in the Bible. Food is prepared in a special way and meat and dairy are served separately. So you can't be kosher and have a cheeseburger. Some unusual Jewish food is beet borscht, gefilte fish, and pickled herring.

Yum, Yum! Many people in China eat many different and unusual things. On a restaurant menu in China, you may find birds' nest soup, snake meat, pigeon, chicken feet, beetles and steamed and braised bear's claw.

Tali held her breath and stared at the animal feet in the bowl.

"What's this?" she asked her friend, Liang.

"Pig's brain soup, just like in China." Liang said, slurping her broth. "My mom made this for International Night. We're lucky she threw in the feet too."

3

"Yuck!"

Tali pushed the bowl away and spilled the soup. "Oops. Sorry."

"I'll get some paper towels," Liang said. "Just get more soup."

Tali coughed and gulped her soda. "Noooooo... thanks. I'm Jewish and I can't eat any meat from a pig."

4

"Sure you can," said Liang, "You're Chinese."

"Your parents adopted you from China, didn't they?"

"But I've lived in America since I was a baby. My family doesn't eat pork."

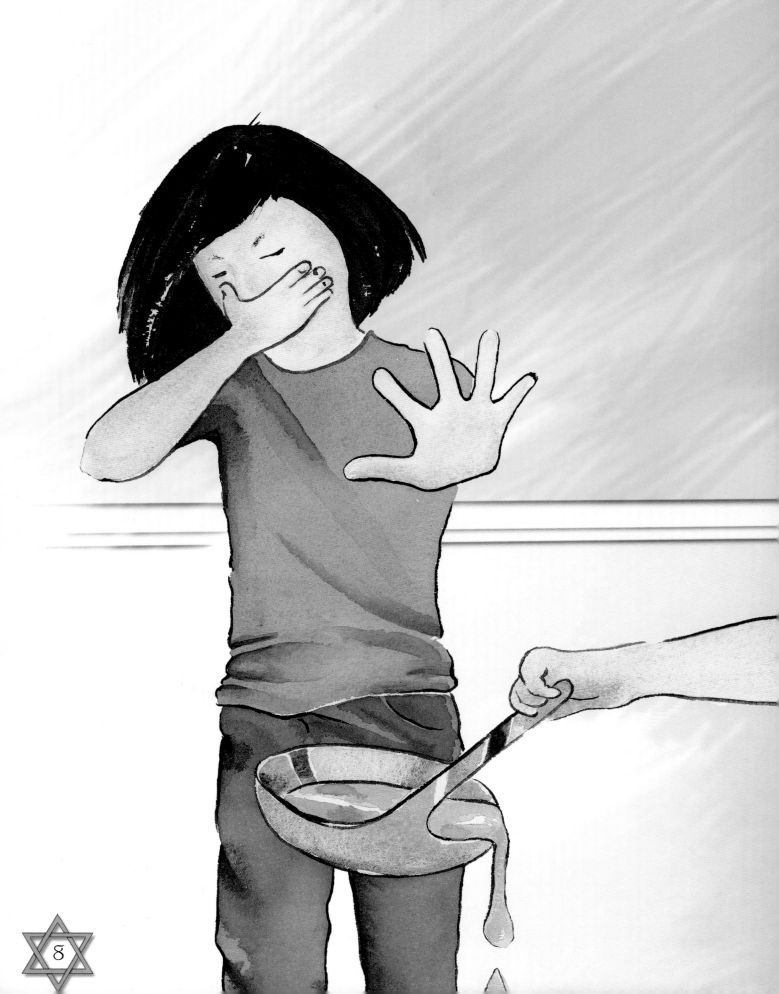

"You were Chinese first," insisted Liang. "Just try it." She dipped out more soup and lifted the spoon to Tali's mouth.

Tali covered her mouth with her hand and shook her head.

"I guess you can't be both Jewish and Chinese," said Liang. "Pick one!"

"If being Chinese means eating that yucky looking soup, I choose Jewish," cried Tali.

The next morning Tali's mom handed her a sack. "Here's a surprise for Show and Tell."

When she got to school, Tali raced to the restroom and peeked into the bag.

"Oh, no, my favorite doll!" She stroked the doll's smooth silk dress. "I chose Jewish so I'm not Chinese anymore."

She shoved the doll behind the trash can and hurried to her classroom. "I'll come back later and get you," she whispered.

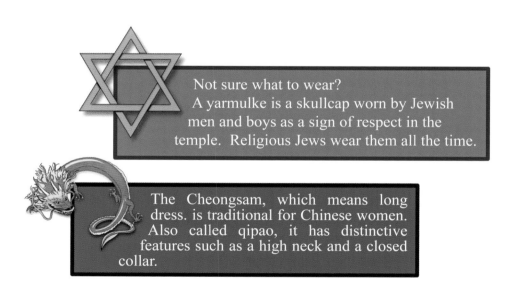

Not sure what to wear?
A yarmulke is a skullcap worn by Jewish men and boys as a sign of respect in the temple. Religious Jews wear them all the time.

The Cheongsam, which means long dress. is traditional for Chinese women. Also called qipao, it has distinctive features such as a high neck and a closed collar.

"You're next, Tali," said the teacher, Ms. Rodriguez.

"I didn't bring anything," Tali muttered.

"Yes, you did, Tali," said Liang. "I found your doll in the restroom!" She tried to hand the doll to Tali.

"That's not mine," Tali lied.

"Yes, it is. Your name is on its foot. Look!"

12

All eyes focused on Tali. Her face turned as red as the doll's skirt.

"My mom made me bring it to school," said Tali. "I don't want to tell the class about it."

"That's fine, Tali," said Ms. Rodriguez. "Let's move on."

Tali snatched the doll from Liang. She whispered to the doll, "I'm so sorry. I still love you," and gently tucked it in her backpack.

As the last bell rang, Ms. Rodriguez reminded the class, "Tonight is International Night. We get to sample food from other countries. Don't forget to wear clothes representing your culture."

Last week Tali had picked out a beautiful new Chinese dress for International Night. But now when she pulled it out of her closet, all she could think about were dancing pigs' feet and a pig's brain.

So Tali grabbed an old dance recital costume and put it on. She tugged at the skirt to pull it down.

She rushed down the hall to her parents' bedroom. She found her father's yarmulke that he always wore to temple and placed it on her head. "This will have to do."

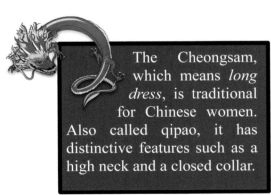

The Cheongsam, which means *long dress*, is traditional for Chinese women. Also called qipao, it has distinctive features such as a high neck and a closed collar.

Not sure what to wear?
A yarmulke is a skullcap worn by Jewish men and boys as a sign of respect in the temple. Religious Jews wear them all the time.

At school, Tali lined up with the other students for the parade of flags.

"Tali, we saved the flags from China for you and Liang," said Ms. Rodriguez.

"Can I carry the Israeli flag instead?" asked Tali.

Ms. Rodriguez glanced at Tali's yarmulke. "Sure you can."

The music started and the children marched into the cafeteria, waving their flags.

The principal walked to the stage. "Your attention, please! Our honored guests from the Chinese Community Center will perform a dragon dance before we eat."

A beautiful Chinese woman stepped up to the microphone. "My name is Ms. Chang.

Would one of the students from China like to lead the dragon dance with me?"

Tali thought about raising her hand, but she didn't. Instead she watched Liang jump to her feet.

"Yes! I want to." said Liang, dashing to the stage where the dragon lay.

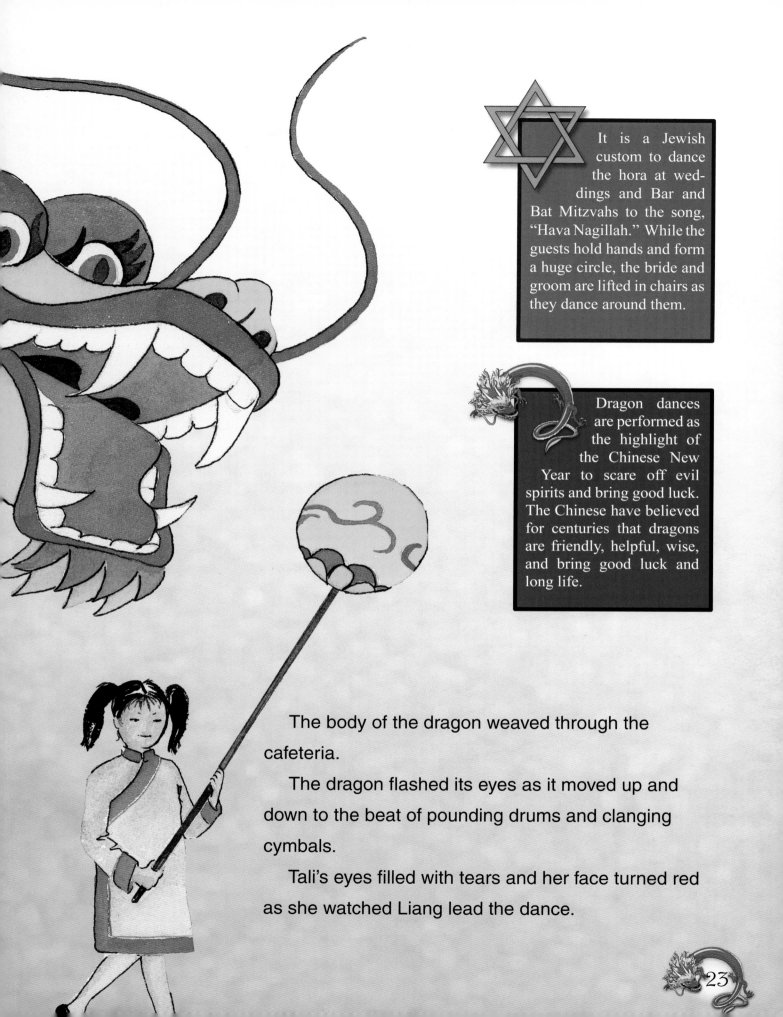

It is a Jewish custom to dance the hora at weddings and Bar and Bat Mitzvahs to the song, "Hava Nagillah." While the guests hold hands and form a huge circle, the bride and groom are lifted in chairs as they dance around them.

Dragon dances are performed as the highlight of the Chinese New Year to scare off evil spirits and bring good luck. The Chinese have believed for centuries that dragons are friendly, helpful, wise, and bring good luck and long life.

The body of the dragon weaved through the cafeteria.

The dragon flashed its eyes as it moved up and down to the beat of pounding drums and clanging cymbals.

Tali's eyes filled with tears and her face turned red as she watched Liang lead the dance.

After the performance, Tali stood in line behind Ms. Chang. The tables were full of foods from many different cultures. Among the foods were cookies, sushi, pizza, tacos, stew, challah, nachos and a big bowl of pig's brain soup.

When they came to the Chinese foods, Liang's mother offered Ms. Chang a bowl of pig's brain soup.

"No, thanks," said Ms. Chang.

"Are you Jewish, too?" asked Tali.

Ms. Chang laughed. "No, I just don't like pig's brain soup."

Tali's eyes grew as big as the bowl of soup and then she giggled. "Me neither."

Tali looked at Liang's mother. "May I have some chicken and rice and a fortune cookie?"

She then took her plate to the Jewish area, "Some latkes with lots of applesauce, please."

Tali sat down with Liang. She tipped her plate back and forth. Applesauce ran onto the rice and sweet and sour sauce ran onto the latkes.

Liang looked at Tali's plate. "Eeew…what are you doing?"

"It's really good together," said Tali with a smile.

Author's Note:

When we adopted our daughter, Hayley, from China, I knew that I wanted to teach her all about her Chinese heritage. It began with her three names. Her Chinese name is Jiang Liangqi (Jiang-last name, Liang-cool and qi-strange). Her American name is Hayley (wide open meadow) Nicolle (victory of the people) Silverman. Her Hebrew name is Sheerah (song) Baruchah (blessed) Devashah (honey and sweetie).

She loves American music and Israeli dancing. From the time she came to America, she made friends from every culture. Since she is a Chinese Jewish American, she celebrates all of the different holidays such as the Chinese New Year, Jewish New Year (Rosh Hashanah), and the American New Year. Ethnic food is her favorite in this order— Mexican, Italian, Chinese and Jewish. Dumplings and matzo ball soup are her favorite Chinese and Jewish foods.

Like many Americans, Hayley is a blend of cultures. So I challenge you to learn about your ancestors—your heritage and celebrate what a marvelous person has come from that "blend." Every culture has beauty, but it is up to each of us to seek and see that beauty in ourselve and others.

Gail

Gail loves foods from every culture. But you won't catch her eating pig's brain soup.

Originally from Nebraska, Gail wrote her first book for her father in third grade. *No Pig's Brain Soup, Please!* is her first published children's book and was the 1st Runner Up in the ABC Children's Picture Book Competition.

Gail has an MBA from the University of Oklahoma and a BS in Social Sciences. After landing her first job in Houston, she stayed and is currently a freelance writer and public relations specialist. Her work has appeared in national and local print, broadcast media and corporate materials. Her publication credits include Love's Journey: A Collage of the China Adoption Experience, Boys' Life, Jack and Jill, Stories for Children, Wee Ones Magazine, and Dogs in the News. Gail, a versatile and award winning writer, is also a produced playwright.

One of her best experiences was traveling to China to adopt her daughter, Hayley. Gail also loves animals and has always had rescued dogs. The current residing king is Bandit, a Shih Tzu, and Hayley the queen. Gail is happy to serve.

Gail is a member of Society for Children's Book Writers and Illustrators.

Lauren is someone who loves her family, enjoys challenges, and likes adventure.

She grew up in a rural area of Canada and for as far back as she remembers, spent countless hours drawing and painting. Following her more practical side, she chose a career in civil engineering, until plans for a family made a field in the visual arts more suitable.

A couple of years after her first child was born, she had quintuplets, so her children definitely took center stage. When her kids went to school she started a business in graphics and web design. Later her family followed an opportunity to move to Texas, which set her career on yet another path—selling cars.

No Pigs Brain Soup, Please! is Lauren's first published children's book.

Pig Brain Soup
in Casserole

Recipe provided by Christy Chang
Houston, Texas

Ingredient A:
1 set Pig brain

Ingredient B:
½ cup Shitake mushroom chopped
½ cup Carrot chopped
½ cup Bamboo shoot chopped
3 oz Sliced chicken or pork
3 slices Sliced ham
¼ cup Onions

Ingredient C:
1 can Chicken broth
1 cup Water
¼ teaspoon Salt
⅛ teaspoon Black pepper
2 tablespoons Cooking wine

Ingredient D:
½ teaspoon Sesame oil
¼ cup Coriander or chinese parsley
¼ cup Green onions
½ teaspoon White pepper

Cooking steps:

1. Clean the pig brain. Remove the soft tissue from the brain and clean with clear water. Soak it in the clear water with 1 tablespoon cooking wine for 10 minutes.

2. Put **Ingredients B** in a casserole and place the pig brain on the top.

3. Mix **Ingredient C** and add them into the casserole. Then steam it for 20 minutes with high heat and medium heat for another 30 minutes.

4. Before serving, you can also add **Ingredient D** to bring up the flavor.

Enjoy the Delicious Pig Brain Soup!!!

I loved it when I was a child. I hope you will love it too.
Christy Chang